damn near

might
still
be

is what it is

damn near might still be is what it is

marcus scott williams

Published By Noemi Press, Inc. A Nonprofit Literary Organization. www.noemipress.org

Cover & Book Design by co•im•press

ISBN: 978-1-934819-06-7

HOW WRETCHED THIS LIFE OF OURS IS!—SO FULL OF FALSE CONCEITS, SO FUTILE, THAT IT IS LITTLE MORE THAN THE SHADOW OF THE CHIMERAS LOOSED BY MEMORY.

—W. G. Sebald, *The Rings of Saturn*

ALL DAY. YOU ALREADY.

—text from my girl Najah

forestburgh ny

dumb lit havent eaten no food. theres a dead mouse squished on the linoleum. sitting outside motionless, tryna actually feel the physical feeling of safety. i hear the distant brook on its marathon over the dad jams. Lily the dogs lookin longingly thoo the screen door. i try to feel the physical feeling of insignificance but everything somehow grounds me and every person around me and my comfortability in these woods says everythings significant somehow. its nice yfm[1]. the dangerous thing about all things is creeping complacency. i'm too lit to be writing. i'm standing in Jeezys big ass army-green jacket actively listening and coolin and not acting weird about it. a bug flies into my eye. up for almost a full 24 at this point.

listening to Black Brook by the fire pit barely outta range of the music, thinking how i'd love to have a house tucked-off someday cuz its essentially building your own personal museum. i aint grow up out in the woods like that so i'm tryna soak up all the auditory sensations while i'm out the city. being surrounded by this many trees is being surrounded by peers; always seen myself as a tree quite literally—color, shape, and the way wind whistles through our branches. a crow in the distance. cargo plane, some shit. Jeezy and John place a rot-blemished door on top of an old coffee table frame. Cat uses a broom to knock off the residual dirt before Jeezy and Mark carry the pieces over underneath the tent. in Shop Rite, remembering when in Walmart checkout lines growing up my Momma would have me and my younger brother tie up all the plastic bags w double knots so nothing spilled out.

[1] yall feel me

i have beautiful city-feet. i turn down a dawn swim to sit quietly outside the cabin and listen to birds tweet from high up snapping branches and the underscoring of Black Brook instead. the tops of pines sway hesitantly. i hit my untitled THC pen and it taste like a lemon jolly rancher. i rest my feet against the fire pit, staring at the ***AMERICA*** Budweiser box w the tagline

FROM THE REDWOOD FOREST TO THE GULF STREAM WATERS
THIS LAND IS MADE FOR YOU & ME

and how thats such a cute idea but how therere people who have very different perceptions of this idea; and moreso how the land wasnt made for nobody as it was pillaged by colonizers and subsequently built by slaves. i stay away from the tree line cuz birds is purging every meal theyve eaten. sections of the dirt clearing are peppered w fine rocks and its soft af against my feet, somehow cleaner than my Bronx apartment floor. dirt dont gotta be synonymous w dirty. i'm using my feet to dig holes, burying them in the dirt to keep cool. sweat twinkles off my body. Black Brook is dumb loud and i'm down here by these digital ferns, crosshatching in the field as far as i can see in a green i could never describe accurately w words. sun sets, silhouettes the pines. we inside our own lil speaker. stars is out tonight. its been awhile since i seen yall whats hannin.

natures brazy—w the exception of birds of prey or birds that caw, all other birds sound like synthesizers. *still smolderin: a memoir*. theres mad bees hovering above the grass circling the fire pit, still still smolderin. me, Combs, Dammy, and Sheela pile in their car and head down 49 Highway. houses peak out from dense forested areas, some sit right off the road prominently, confidently. theres heavy, ambivalent clouds in a pure blue sky that reminds me of the fluff Petunia the dog tore outta that stuffed animal on the bed as i fell into sleep last night. some clouds cast impossible shadows onto Bear Mountain.

MY TIME LAVISH

—Desiigner

sometimes its mudpuddles

i fight off exhaustion against my Frontier flights window seat. tryna sleep the whole shit so i can be rested and maybe not fuck up Rich Homies lil REM since i'm getting in mad early. i take a shuttle to Avis to pick up a rental car. one of the guys at the counter is dumb sardonic, on some Bickle from *Taxi Driver* type shit. he holds me down w a free upgrade for putting up w his humor. a *feel me* sticker is outside the side entrance to Rich Homies brib.

Denver is way hotter than i expected, as if i'm pressed to the atmosphere and its just like the suns right up on a nigger. 'what time is it sir?' from this disheveled presumably homeless person. 'uhhhh 8:25.' its really 8:26, then i follow up by saying 'have a good day man.' i remember the barista face at Port Side and cant remember if i had a crush on them in February, yet the way we catch eyes makes it seem as if i or maybe Oolong had flirted w them back when. could just be this sexy ass outfit on me: black skinny jeans stuck to the hairs on my thighs w that pink mesh dress tied at my waist in a way that makes it ride up, hips cuttin, every tattoo on my torso and my extremely small, Hershey Kiss nipples plainly visible. puffy monuments saunter over the mountains to the west. Julius Eastmans *Stay On It* and the live version of Velvet Undergrounds *New Age* at Maxs Kansas City are soundtrack highlights of this drive to Angel Fire. its disconcerting how green the mountains are up close. bobcats rip boulders outta cliffsides and the highways consolidate lanes. a yellow road sign w a black moose on it. a few miles ahead the landscape disappears into a heathery grey—you can see the rain hours before it hit if your view is unobstructed. the state motto, *The Land of Enchantment*, resonates thoo Cimarron Canyon. swerving slowly as to not hydroplane, the canyons peaks got my neck rubbery. thoo Eagles Nest, 10 miles outside Angel Fire, i'm hit w buttery nostalgia. this place is more beautiful than the memories i held for it. wide patches of lavender and sumn yellow i cant quite identify spring from around bushes, looking like an A$AP Rocky video gone terribly terribly right. fog permeates from the pines like *whoa*[2]. hills rolling into future mountains. drive out to me and Ricks old house to the sound of some Beach House b-sides. someones using the property much better than we did. theres

---

[2] RIP

a new lil uglasss shack some yards from the house and an RV coolin next to that and the shack out back looks redone or repaired. its so funny that this rental car has Missouri plates. some things i cannot escape.

the next morning approaching Taos on 64 thoo Carson National Forest. ***ELK CROSSING AREA*** signs as well as ***COW CROSSING*** signs. cars are annoyed that i'm taking curves so slowly so they pass in **DO NOT PASS** zones which is fine cuz i'm also dangerously snapping pictures for all my group chats. some pines have roots that claw out the trunk kinda like my dreads do out my scalp. when Rick and i see each other for the first time in over a year we hug for an tiny eternity, chat w goofy smiles on our faces. she combs knots out her blond hair w an afropick. 'have you seen me since i got dreads?' 'have you seen how long my hair is?!' she hops into the shower and i make me, her, and her wife some coffee. i hug her wife the same way. i'm happy for Rick. i'm told stories about Rick feeding her wife caramel popcorn in her sleep, about how pokeable her face is. we paint our nails and they show me around their Airbnb. lil pueblo house tucked off a side street w an impossibly narrow driveway, a skylight in the kitchen yellowing the house, a spiral staircase leading to the bedroom overlooking the living room. on the way to the wedding ceremony in Angel Fire i have to pull off and piss and keep snapping Taos Canyon. thinking about the *Revisionist History* episode when Malcolm Gladwell briefly mentioned transactive memory and if that translates to us leaving memories in the media we're incessantly compiling. if when the photo dies so dies the memory. tryna internalize my surroundings so i can recall this scenery of my own volition. i lead people to the backyard where the reception space at Ricks parents' request, meet Ricks Cajun grandmother. i meet two new young people round my age and i wanna take em around green places in NYC and go hiking w them in New Mexico. Anita is just as beautiful as she was since i last seent her four years ago. shes got sunflowers for eyes. she is affectionate w me in such a specifically friendly way that i think she may have inspired my own affections. its great to be around people who aint from New York City. that place is feels like a jail cell sometimes. accents carve smileys across my cheeks. the pines smells fresh and i take deeper breaths eeemno its harder to maintain steady breathing at this altitude. weddings are much different when you care about the people getting married. i smoke a poorly rolled joint w Andrew. 'its so nice to have the sun to tie back.'—English is not this random persons first language, not the way she fumbles over that *r*. Rick sits me and Anita to her right. tears migrate into my facial hair. champagne is popped and i participate in the ritual eeemno i quit drinking last year. funny cuz i'm poured a really short glass like they knew. to like be amongst trees again *fuuuuuuck*. me, Andrew, and Cal sip the rest of the joint and talk about mindfulness and how we as young people need to live in-moment because of its tangibility. i describe what i'm writing to them. we hug each other genuinely. i make the dangerous mistake of driving too high thoo dark dusk mountains that fight over whether to be bloody orange or inky tussin-purple. theres a shock when you realize what and whomst is outside your bubble, corny as that may sound. lets get it poppin. i cant help but recall totaling my Isuzu Rodeo fifty miles outside of town a few years ago. youll never really understand a song until you play it outside its intended sphere and see how shit feels soundtracked by it. i always dream so vividly at damn near 11,000 feet above the motherfucking sea!

my ears stay popping at 10,000 shout outs to Bobcat Pass. clouds lookin like Zeus and nem banishing shadows against the mountain range. driving thoo San Luis in Colorado heading back from the wedding and I only see that theres nothing but maybe one restaurant and strips of closed businesses and abandoned buildings. the white people are dumb friendly at the gas station and smile at me. cranky af after being in a car for too many hours and aint eaten and damn sober. Rich Homie tats code on his fingers and gives me a Meatwad tattoo. we ride over to the Safeway bumping Drakeo the Ruler. *understand that its regular.*

sneezin like fut but it feels good cuz i'm clearing all my sinuses out. i hear a <bird> in a tree trillin. i wanna pick some of this wild lavender but its currently being pollinated. let these bees live they lives. in the Five Points neighborhood where Rich Homie lives, developers are building "luxury rentals" faster than ive ever seen shit spring up. theres mad homeless people in the area due to the three shelters in the vicinity. having a safe place to be is a luxury so i'm not sure what da fut deez developers talmbout. mad sleepy after dropping off the rental to the airport in addition to taking the train back into the city. take lil nap. need to kill 10 hours, waiting for an old friend to meet up who lives in Boulder for dinner. i have to get gelato and duck into a movie theater to escape the heat. outsides much cooler cuz of what looks like rain coming. 'eh what is that? oh its a dead flower not a bug.' texting and walking is difficult. my Precious Amazonians eyes are just as big as i remember, and i'm reminded we can be really goofy-serious together. we talk about open relationships and tethering to people and having several soulmates. *young nigger livin now fut what da future sayin.* there are orange beetles jumping along patches of lilted-yellow grass that PA describes as having wings and also being crunchy. the sun sets, we get stoned on the last loose-booty joint i have, enjoy a few moments of silence. she hums near inaudibly. we hug at Union Station w an *i love you.* i sneak into the train to Denver International w the same ticket i copped in the morning. i'm really feeling a way. iont wanna be leaving this air no matter how stuffy the pollen got me. my default emotion right now is loneliness, but it doesnt feel like conventional lonelyism at this particular moment. left nostril closed off. a salty face got my glasses greasy. iont know why i have such an issue w feeling undesirable but its an hideous feeling. theres nothing worse than an airport w every shop closed. i'm slinking absently under fluorescent lights and LED screen panels reflecting their double off the linoleum.

joblessness

directly above the red FLUSH button the wall of the bus bathroom is broken like a crooked smile, like half the face thats tryna hold a cigar between its teeth. no flush came from pushing the button. neither my USB port nor the outlet are functional so i have to shut off my—

me and Mai walk to the beach to watch the sunrise after dropping off my bags at her crib. theres a cloud party along the horizon thats blocking the sun so we settle, snugg on a blanket close to the purring Atlantic and discover shapes in the party. theres a dog right above the bright spot; therere ninja turtles; theres a tongue whipping out from the same bright spot mockingly. it starts to sprinkle and i have to piss so we walk back to the apartment. talking about my parents and how emotional home is for me. RIP Miss Danita. an unfortunate consequence of having younger parents is knowing their friends and watching them watch them pass and how you have to watch the people that raise you grapple w feelings theyve never understood prior. a lil nap is needed. new rap name: Lil Dreaming of You. i hear the wind being redirected under jet engines. i'm in a Walmart in Virginia buying womens floral-print keds, alternately making out w Mai and browsing aisles. living in NYC you forget how people really be out in the world looking-feeling-speaking. Mai takes me to a cozy spiritual enlightenment conversation at some Malaysian teachers home. he talks about the ego. i think about the ego as a sponge and how environmental it is. 'how do you use your ego?' as children we like play-conscious, Mai and i theorize, high, but having an ego is an essential function in the human experience, as of course your environment plays a starring role in socialization and development. i use my ego as a reflecting tool, not necessary to outwardly learn a lesson yet to be open to learning lessons and asking questions. fuck *meaning* its all relative to your beliefs and surroundings my nigger you do what you need to do.

theres metallic wailing coming from cicadas outside the window. we lay in bed, sticky af, talking about the logistics of covering their exoskeletons in carnauba wax. something so stimulating about consistent screen-scrolling. whenever i leave a job i get temporarily addicted to combing Craigslist. the cicadas are shaving aluminum whilst a neighbor whacks weeds. we pack carrots and kale and sliced turkey to go to First Landing State Park. we decide to hit the Cape Henry Lighthouse first which unbeknownst to the two of us is located on a military base. Mai doesnt fw authority so shes mad uncomfortable as officers search her car, check her license, detail what locations are picture appropriate. (i wanna whisper to him, 'fuck the surveillance state bruh.') the lighthouse is a mile and a half from the entry point. we browse the gift shop at the ground level and i consider getting a magnet for my Grandma, a lighthouse trinket for my boy Deadbody, or a copy of the constitution to scribble over. the obviously ex-military cashier is annoyed when iont wanna donate for renovations because i wanna read more into it first, is that okay *damn*. the base of the lighthouse is encircled by a low wooden fence and invasive, unknown flora. we climb up and i'm dumb winded but its worth it to touch the original brick and to see the sea splash against stone barriers along the beach thats **FOR MILITARY FAMILIES ONLY**. the bronze has oxidized into a dark seafoam w lil rust-crusted slashes of amber. the lighthouse is the first federal building built in the United States. i wonder if slaves built this shit. (i know the answer). she shows me the Edward Cayce place where she works and we get iced coffee at a discount and meet some coworkers who recommend paths to walk; these paths are six miles deep into the park and i'm just not w that shit today. we walk by Lake Susan Constant and park on the sand, make out, build breadless sandwiches. branches dip toes in the water. *butterfly boolin: a memoir*. unidentified claw marks in drying mud. bridge over the marsh. loose one-off beer cans. walk along the beach and lower our ankles in ocean. got *I'm A Nasty Hoe* by Ugly God on repeat between the ears. (if you fwm[3] you know i eat fast af): theres an army of food slithering into my stomach. the tide high and gentle, the sand disintegrates under our feet. the water rushes in and glides out carrying lil black faces, and sometimes the whiteness of the bubbles resemble static breaking. i'm mystified by how the music of the Atlantic damn near supersedes these fucking military jets. fireworks on the beach cancelled due to rough sea conditions.

[3] fuck with me. *fw* is simply fuck with, by the way. i know ive used that a few times in here already. i be forgetting yall may not know me, or are aged enough to need context.

tfw you gotta apply for hella jobs. multiple a day type shit. i'm not worried this time. the NYC job hunt game is no fucking joke—i'm coming in w shooters on me. vegetable spaghetti in the backyard before walking over to the Virginia Museum of Contemporary Art. a bridge over marshland w tall stalks of weeds leads away from the museum, eventually feeding back into sidewalkless streets. i find what i think is a carcass of a cicada on the first sidewalk outside a group of project houses that Mai encourages me to keep but we think it may be alive, its still soft when i pet its underside and maybe it moves very subtly so i toss it back into the grass so cuzz can stay cool and recover. sun oppresses. fail finding justifiably cheap swimming trunks for tonight. i'm touching my dick in Mai bed while shes at meetings for two hours. she forgot to vacuum like she promised herself yesterday so i do some light dusting around the ceiling fan blades. the window projects a perfect rectangle of sunshine against the drab olive sheets. my dick has reddish undertones and is currently half-flaccid. when she comes back we cuddle hard af for an hour. i ask her to close her eyes so i can see the pink veins bolting across her eyelids. she gives me a deep massage. its hard to wanna get up for any activity. on the beach we open this combo tub of pico and guacamole aaand are bummed that we were tricked into believing there would be equal amounts of each. skys fuschia and blood orange. the ocean is black at the horizon. she tells me about her ex she recently broke off w and the relationship they had; about their house in Vermont that belonged to his family, about his addictions and traumas and how they affected her, about her decades-long infatuation w him and starting her real real life. i pick up sweet potato fries cuz yfm its me thank you and we navigate thoo darkness under magnolia trees and chorusing crickets and headlights imitating searchlights eavesdropping on our conversations. i tell her its hard to call my parents rn because theyre both having such a hard time separately. Dad got fucked over for his disability check after an on-the-job accident shattered a disk in his back. Momma best friend just passed, a best friend w which i grew up seeing at damn near every function and had a personal relationship. i hope they can sense me thinking about them, always am. i hold back tears tryna get sentences out. they are great parents to me. like yeah they mightve subconsciously twerked me and my little brother up by getting divorced but no parent doesnt fuck up a kid. lowkey part of the process. we never got whooped w switches though. this definitely has an tiny effect on my desire to never start a family. Mai gives me tarot reading that i identify w. i ask a question about my future employment and other opportunities. my path card is all about my process of healing, being supported at the same damn time yet needing to heal. iont need a full time job. the Ace of Cups tells me i'll have fruitful experiences in freelance work. my ambition is holding me back; i need to let the seeds i planted grow and not worry about managing their growth, just nurture them like only i can do.

i look into Mai smile, the way she opens the left side of her mouth so slightly to reveal only three top teeth is hard to pull away from. plan on hitting Target for a bathing suit after breakfast but its raining lowkey kinda hard but we go anyway cuz all my nails dumb long and i need clippers to avoid anxiously eating them. get caught in a lil light capitalism while up in there: spray bottle for dry plants; a cassette aux; spearmint gum. i get angry when we drive off realizing i left the clippers at the counter. i cant place the angers origins. maybe angry because its a stupid thing to be so aloof w my shit, cuz bruh i'm now unemployed so i *haaaave* to go back to grab them or issa waste. angry cuz i'm getting angry in front of someone i like and dont want them to change their opinion of me. objectively, the anger is prolly blossoming from loss of control. cant reign in these emotions, embarrassed that i feel everything on Ten. i get angry tryna print a bus ticket at the public library cuz i *haaaaaave* to get a library card and pay .20¢ to print but it doesnt print out correctly so i *haaave* to run back to reception to ask the librarian—whomst complimented my freeforms—to put another quarter on my account and select the exact words i want printed. all this running back and forth like i'm Aaliyah. a cicada dive bombs into my hair and bounces off into the grass. i scream, 'YO FUCK OFFA ME NIGGER,' apologize fervently to Mai, who offers to do a quick reading to figure out where this all stems from. 'its probably that—this is just my opinion—that when youre the only person you believe in you feel helpless when something happens that can lead to all this anxiety.' (*anxiety*! *control*!) its humid af sans showers. we bontemplate the beach or kayaking or blacklight mini golf. she pushes me to meditate for one minute like my girl KCV has in the past. i'm afraid i wont do it correctly but i get comfortable and close my eyes, try losing myself. at first i'm a lil anxious. the air under the jets or her turning pages or the pieces of carrot hanging in my throat are major distractions. i use my ADHD to my advantage: i allow myself to think a million thoughts, give myself infinite paths to progress, until when i check outside stimuli w the epiphany that i'm disconnected from it, partially from body. minutes fade and later i see the stress plastering my face in a picture Mai took. after laying on the beach for awhile, i run out to dunk my head in the ocean, blinded on resurfacing by a savory burning penetrating my eyeballs. dehydrated skin makes it so we stuck together. 'do you think i crave salty chips because they reminds me of the ocean?' barnacles of rust reef the Fun Party bathroom dividers. the ocean is black from the top of the ferris wheel. she sings a song about an outside cat we met earlier in the day. i subconsciously try to suppress telling her i'll miss her for the thousandth time. we laugh about the picture of geese in her room. she thanks me for coming. 'now we know each other.' we talk a lil more about her ex: when she approached me in Tompkins Square Park back in May and asked for my number, she was fresh off the relationship, bravely tryna look for a distraction. 'glad i can be your tool for that.' her slight-smile. i look at her across her room as she orders me a Lyft. outside us and her roommate talk about forgetting how to be a tourist here when youre living inside the attraction. eating fudge on the boardwalk, the ferris wheel, the storytellers and buskers w tiny handmade guitars. my Lyft driver from Chicago and turns out he grew up in Logan Square. we talk about the Blue Line and how much its been gentrified. he reminisces to me about the graffiti youd see, tells me about his time in the military, about a dirty bunkmate. i think about Mai, sitting within this strip mall, waiting for the bus back to NYC to pull up. i can hear the club popping thoo the paper thin bathroom walls of the New York Bus terminal. the bus is dumb crowded, i relinquish my seat for a mother and her kids. somehow theyre assigning seats but like when that policy come into effect? only a few of the outlets and USBs are operational and my new seat is not one of them. circles circles circles circles circles.

in exchanges

stay sucking on my tongue which is a problem this very moment cuz of a canker sore on the roof of my mouth. the foam earplugs are a similar color to my earwax just less toasty. half-dreaming about the plane doing circles and half-nightmaring three separate planes nosediving. this my mandatory time to thinkaboutdyin. underneath us the scenery is flat and carved into squares like lemon bars. i force-stop myself from rolling my eyes when this group from Long Island talk about going straight to Overland Park. they cant believe that some of the houses are *so big!* i joke w Stunna on the way back from the airport about his disdain for biscuits and its funniest cuz he dont fw em off the strength of him appearing more country than he believes himself to be. we chop it up on my Momma back patio cuz she tore up the basement carpet after all the flooding Kansas City been having. she not home yet. new mirror in the bathroom. napping in the guest bedroom. all i hear is a choir of cicadas breaking in and out, the twisting of the ceiling fan, the squeaking dryer in the basement. Stabler whispers on 2. Momma knocks and i greet her w a hug and kiss on the cheek. leaving Raytown down 87th, speeding, a lil distracted by the lusciousness; theres not a human being alive that can suppress this muscle memory, this drive and the ancient details from my childhood ingrained like sand up in my dreadlocks. zonin whilst driving. a false sky. i abstain from a $2 burrito because i ate Mommas chicken and noodles. me and Oolong talk about his new photos and how we been on the same waves since we met my junior year of high school. the word *BLACK* is mentioned mad times in the essay about his work from an upcoming group show. listening to beats Macy traded for some weed. now i'm dumb lit tryna stay bognizant. cicadas on-the-beat i hear you; i'm followin. saffron-light drippin on leaves making them thangs look like hot gold. iont think theres ever been shit on Troost between Cleaver and Brush Creek Blvd. Gates is forever. *NAACP!* supertitles the starless cobalt when i realize i'm driving in Missouri. got *The Negro Motorist Green Book* saved as a PDF in my phone. the commercials at this hour are saved strictly for Proactiv or live XXX chatrooms.

the bathroom mirror in my Momma house favors my rib lines and wraps shadows across my collarbone. sleep was trash cuz i'm really starting to worry about income and i think my last employer tryna hatefully block my unemployment and like how imma pay rent? my Grandma sitting on the porch of her new apartment building off Bellefontaine in her orange Obama shirt. moved from her house out in the 50s that she been in for like 30 years. i rinse my mouth out w hydrogen peroxide to quell these cankers. *NBC ACTION NEWS MIDDAY* on her flat screen, boomin. photos of cousins, my Momma, both Grandparents, lil cousins, aunties, uncles, my lil brother, and 7 pictures of me are hanging from nails on her living room walls. listening to my lil cousin D talk about her slumber party. 'we played Twister, we played hide-and-go-seek outside, we played tag outside, we played Uno, we played Connect 4 ...' see my big cuzzo Dar Dar for the first time in a grip. he used to babysit me and my lil brother. i got the *THUGGIN* tattoo on my right forearm for him; he introduced me to E-40 and stick-and-pokes, to UGKs *Dirty Money* and Cee-Lo first album. he dreaded up now too, almost 40. when he tells me the last time he was in NYC they were mad rude to him i tell him he should stay tf outta Times Square next time. when i slink off i see him again down the street and i wanna smoke w him but my other lil cuzzo there, and i'm fervently against smoking in front of children. 'be safe cuzzo—and get on that bus!'—my lil one cant understand why i'd wanna walk the two miles into the Crossroads. The Grove Park is empty underneath alllis humidity and each dolo tree slaps wide capes of shadow across its field. after Oolong show, squad poppin out at Chez Charlies and i drink a beer for the first time in over a year. boolin loose boolin. me and Jer talk about being sober. both of us havent drank inna grip. i feel him, he loves getting fucked up and partying and theres some of his best nights in there but he decided that life is just as tight as fuzzing-out. i feel for you family. life is so fucking wild. i'm thinking of the lavender fields in Angel Fire. i'm thinking of this hurricane hitting Texas rn. duuuumb loose. a text:

> *the price of my Uber home is about half of what i thought it was gonna be cuz my momma lives deep in the suburbs kinda. i had the first beer I've had since like July 2016 tonight I'm like it's weird to feel it like that sorta looseness that i haven't felt for so long. & I'm dumb nostalgic being w old friends & the artists that i miss fw & speaking to, i feel strange, being home makes me brazy emotional. & it surprises me every time & like the deadness in the wind blowing thoo the cx-9 windows hits my ears so familiarly. the fact that i eeem refer to it as home is really telling of my subconscious feelings towards this place yfm. this ride down Gregory Blvd is off because I'm not in the driver's seat. i think nostalgia doesn't have to be such an awful feeling, like it doesn't haven't to be such a yearning to return home.*

i'm tryna keep the nostalgia for Kansas City fucking decadent because when i come back i'm tryna have that shit push my shoulders to the ground cuz its so unique so like why would i wanna ruin that feeling? its a singular feeling for a place i never called *home*. makes coming inland not as desolate as the Coasts would have you believe. when you see the wildlife and rolling green hills and you smell the overgrown weeds reaching outta sidestreets, why would you not fw Missouri? texts to the *Real Barl Thomas Hours* group chat:

> *has one beer & is smacked.*

eeem a lil alcohol makes me feel nauseous. like the fluids in my skull are turbulent.

therere a few dusty particles in my day-old coffee on the nightstand. my lil cadences exactly like mine. riding south on 435 to 71 out to Dads in Grandview. talmbout the *Final Fantasy X* remaster and how hard getting the ultimate weapons is and some dark Aeon that gets summoned in Zanarkand now. helping Dad pick up some furniture gifted to him. surprise! Belton Missouri has had some development but its suburban cookie cutter shit like a Qdoba and Panda Express and Kay Jewelers. Walmart and Wendys beeeeen out here. eating Godfathers Pizza. my Godfather Robert comes thoo to fwm. 'were you high while you were writing it?' in reference to my first book. 'yeah, ha, most of the time.' him and my Dad talking about growing up in the 30s and which blocks banged harder than others. fortunate to have family that knows i'm out here gettin fut up fut up and trust me to live my truth. so fortunate my Momma will let me scoop her newish car at 2300 and trust me to whip her whip until 0300. Oolongs painting skills have leveled up. scoop the crew to drive down to Boy Bois *Alter Birth* party. people are finding their own rhythms: dancing w babies shout outs Drakeo, cute queers in diapers and pink wigs, rampant rolling up in the club. somehow theres always sumn poppin when i come back to the city, albeit only twice a year i come back. eating pistachios w gang outside on fox-washed skreets. i ask a white person of consequence what this place is and i get a non-answer answer so i guess i can go fuck myself. theres a dude getting domed off a loading dock hollering at the moon. shout out to Stunna complimenting my driving by calling it calming. ground turkey taco salad in my Momma brib. certain shit dont ever change; certain shit dont have no business changing.

Stunnas an anti-biscuite. everybody working in PTs is forlorn. i'm about to experience that post-rain Mizzuruh humidity. (only niggas from Kansas pronounce it that way.) Salvation Army and Thou Mayest Coffee are closed because everybodys at church on Sundays. i cant feel compelled to write in these sentimental conditions. 'the raggedier he is the more he likes it.'—my Grandma in reference to me.

these are big, big facts.

iam here, somewhere in the sun

THE BASED GODS PRAYER

tfw stress grippin the back of that neck
i'm like fuck up offa me
all this unfurling of fingers got me meditating
Based God hear my prayers: i pray for the following while i'm out in Europe:

safe passage to London
a couch or bed to sleep on
that the $14.99 i paid for Tinder Gold proves fruitful
that i get wet up as a result
the kindness of strangers
some wisdom from strangers
to not get kidnapped or Blacknapped
that the measly money i have to my name stretches
to sell some books for some road cash
to find a reliable weed connect
for nimble, steady fingers to learn rolling joints
to make at least one new long-lasting friendship
to strengthen pre-existing friendships
to discover new music that makes me feel sumn
to learn something valuable about cultures separate from my own
to practice patience

we shall see what fuck going on,
its movement thats necessary

German Words Learned

danke—thank you
garten—garden
sehr gut—very good
bitte—please
bussi—kiss

Italian Words Learned

grazie—thank you
salute—cheers
prego—youre welcome
per favore—please
bello—beautiful
carino—kind
vorrei—may i please have

Crucial Travel Items (Remembered)

passport
downloaded maps from Google Maps
translation app and offline dictionary

Crucial Travel Items (Forgotten)

scarf
a winter coat
white skin
warm socks
more money

. . . BUT LONELINESS IS A SURGICAL THING.

— *me*

i wonder why my hands need to be buried when i'm tryna sleep.

skkr

i cant tell if the irregular splashing is from the dishwasher or the ever-present rain pummeling the plastic roof covering the skylight. i pull Adderall out bunched up black socks with no intention of poppin none yet. the negative space between buildings is always the most telling. sound and water are trapped. vibrative vortex. pipes produce synthetic fresh air. inaccessible. its the place i go to when i want to be completely alone. the bricks are grey which has the green mildew like fuck it up fuckitupfuckitup *yuh*—its sorta cold and the changing seasons got me shivering, hoping my body acclimates.

skkr

i wake up forgetting i'm in another country, Ibizan hound in my face in a playful position. i decide to put the dishes in the dishwasher cuz its literally the least i can do to repay Stonys hospitality. play *Kill La Kill* on the projector and text KCV about some trouble shes having. theres runs in my black leggings. fighting thoughts and feelings against cold weather to go explore the neighborhood. i get a long black coffee at Wilton Way Cafe where London Fields Radio is situated. DJ is playing some lo-fi jazzy beats. perfect for chillin and/or studying. text-storms from Tinder and WhatsApp. i'm reminded that no matter where you are in the world, connection is key. a capital *r* Romantic thought, but cathartic nonetheless.

skkr

why must you state a purpose when entering a country? why must i know what i'm doing at every turn? why yall watching me? iont know and couldnt reliably tell you why i'm here; i'll figure that lil shit out day by day or a few years from now as i'm re-reading these notes yfm.

skkr

i feel comfortable in London—is this because ive been before? because issa Western country? because i speak English? thoughts stab me, in recognition of the wonderment in people staring at my hair, wondering if they would describe it as "funny" or "cool". as i'm walking back to Stonys flat my muscles tense cuzza cold weather. mans plead w me for change for food. 'anything please. its an emergency.' his eyes tellin me he not lying yet i'm still like, naw. theres some guilt. if there wasnt the omnipresent fear of running out of money during this trip i would definitely have been more inclined to throw him £2. is that a good excuse? excuse is excuse regardless of how i justify it for myself. the Tubes got me all fut up, so much so that i'm afraid to pop my earbuds in for fear of missing a stop and paying eeem more than i have in my pocket. fuck a Zone. i do really wanna listen to *In Too Deep* by Trippie Redd on repeat. deadass i'm reminded though that i'm an experienced traveller so once i solidify these lil directions between the ears, aint no prblems. get off at Piccadilly Circus and walk to White Horse Pub for a pint. waiting on John. *yoooo* i definitely stand out. i notice this while on the train boppin, wishing my dreads were longer so i can look a lil mo ignit and *haaadem* thangs swangin. thinking about how its vibrant and touristy in Piccadilly and iont wanna take photos to be that type of nigger, but i'm tryna get over that cuz i feel a responsibility to get pictures for the family so they can live vicariously thoo my experiences. i wanna do that for them.

skkr

TWO GREAT IDEAS

great aesthetic idea:

start using footnotes but instead of numbers use only exclamation marks

sample idea:

sample the sound of me writing in this notebook w this Pentel Hybrid Technica 0.5mm

skkr

spent £10 that iont have to go to a party w some of Stonys friends. Noemi is Arctic stripper chic at the suits and gowns party. meet Martine Syms and *gave* her a copy of my first book; in the back of my sweaty ass neck i'm thinking *look cuh you cant be giving shit out you need to make some gwop while you out here.* me to me: *social capital got you this far, bleed.* have to strip my shirt off, hot af in this club. i think because of the anticipated amount of social anxiety i forget how much i do love dancing. a hot ass party feels good in this fucking cold. babes breh fuuuuuck and yall know its easy for a nigger to crush up on someone. Noemis confidence is mad attractive and like i would have to strap myself in and plant these muuhfuckin feet. walk back to Stonys under a full moon peepin at a nigger from underneath graveyard-shift clouds. its projecting a rainbow ring and i'm like, *my nigger stop tryna flex.* do **NOT** think about money. think about you having a good time. be proud that you didnt hit Your Story once because you were busy boppin. i see Noemi on the walk back, climbing the few front steps into her flat. i express interest in kicking it some more. 'see you soon.' are the words people say as goodbyes binding? i tell Deadbody imma just start nonthreateningly tellin people i'm tryna fuck but whens really an appropriate time for allat. w wrist upturned in defeat towards the moon, shit iont know. cars sound the same on all roads. leaves gingerly scratch the sidewalk. theres a pink rhinestone heart pasty on my cheek in lieu of a face tattoo. i'm hoping my hormones get some relief in the next few days. shadows dancing on my own like T-Pains *BIG ASS CHAIN* diamonds. shut down Google Maps for the challenge. my shadow improves each day. i almost like it more than my face frfr. this day two but dont think about money yet.

skkr

SOUNDS OF HACKNEY, CHILLY IN NOVEMBER

accented laughter in the open-air market. Tube in the distance like a muted mechanical banshee. Cocteau Twins in Donlon Books.

'is it the crazy woman?'

a beautiful voice coming from whomstever has this beautiful pitbull on a lead. reading Frank Oceans writing in his *i-d* spread and it fucked up my perceptions temporarily. i think, permanently, of words permanently. (i think he would like my writing.) cheek warmth.

'any four pots are five!'

(*East London accent.*)

'i'll take fifteen quid!'

auctions out the ass.

'fiver! stolen orchids! these are all nicked!'

strong-smelling lavender. a lulling grumble to the crowd. PATIENCE as a theme flashing before my eyes. everything very bright yellow shout outs my sun. ghostly-white bikeriders. a chill down my spine not from the cold but from forgetting that i was in another country and almost getting clapped by a car. constant barking throughout the meadows.

skkr

wake up refreshed if not a bit cold. me and Stony share a coffee, talk about his dogs origins; how he wasnt originally Stonys dog but an exs, and over a period he was sorta left up to Stony to foster. dog is so cute, even when it vomits on the hardwood flooring. Tinder match hits me. we make explicit plans to meet Monday. todays finna be sloooow. Stony and i talk about the differences between tinctures and essential oils, he shows me sets hes bought and homemades of both. mugwort to elderberry to oil of oregano (that i drop under my tongue) to other shit i cant remember post-pack post-shower. Stony and i have a similar view of the past. its all an abstraction lowkey. rosemary stimulating the brain and hair. i revel in some English Lavender essential oil before a serious conversation about the spirits of plants. i tell him that theres an increase in my generations interest in caring for plants because like social media connects us—met Stony via Instagram thoo my girl Cheyenne, who i met in the Bronx—but also can and does leave us socially and emotionally isolated in novel ways, so caring for these plants really impacts our mental health. theres real connectivity, deepens empathy. he talks about the effectiveness of caring for something in very uncomplicated ways—sunlight, water, attention. he talks about Western perceptions of medicine as being used to treat a problem once its already bad or as a fixative; these oils and tinctures have a hippie dippie ass connotation and eeen if they dont work theres real value in a sort of placebo that at least opens your brains perception to a wider universality. we talk a lot about fighting against a capitalist system and if making small changes work on a small scale. we resolve that small steps *do* make a difference, you put it in the universe, shit be incremental, we can only do our best. a story about doing our best that nearly brings anime-fat tears up outta him: theres a rainstorm and all the animals in the forest run down to the river for protection. a hummingbird quickly flies to the river for a droplet of water just to return to a flower and place the droplet in it to save it. the other animals question this, heckle the hummingbird. the hummingbird replies, 'all you can do is your best.' effort is everything.

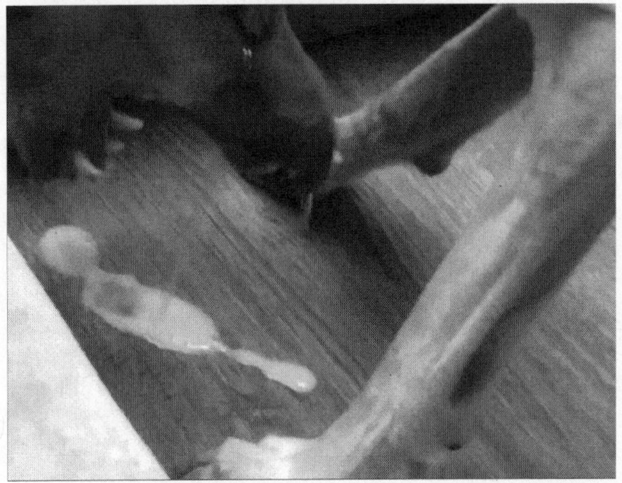

skkr skrr

think about how i like a rule of threes when making comparisons. like, an A to B comparison is banal and unidirectional when an A to B to C comparison challenges the whole system without there being too many points to muddy the larger picture. like instead of A vs B its A vs B vs C or AB vs C or A vs BC or AC v B or whathaveyou, a nice wide but contained debate. giving enough without giving too much yfm.

skkr

thinking about how climaxing is considered the end all be all. i want the dramatic structure around relationships to be just as enthralling as the climax. the introduction is approached all tepid cuz youre meeting for the first time and tryna impress one another; the rising action is the conversation and getting to know somebody, hanging out, which only enhances the climax because you can identify and relate to that person on a deeper level, your perception of them changes obvi but if i'm like fucking just to get a nut off i'd definitely be using the other person strictly as a vessel, which i'm against cuz hittin it real quick bussin and dippin feels duuumb empty; the climax is clearly the climax; the falling action is that post-coital snuggling, that body-on-body heat thats incomparable to anything else, hearing somebodys softly rising and falling breath is also so intimate i'm embarrassed by it a lil bit; the resolution is whatever that relationship develops into.

skkr

i just tried to shake my dreads and deadass a leaf wafted and fell to the bathoom floor. i can hear the fan in the bathroom oscillating, imitating my heartbeat.

skkr.

didnt feel like writing yesterday, felt like living. highlights from yesterday: all day i was tripping over thinking about the kindness of strangers. i walk around Croydon in bitter ass cold w Chicago-style winds w Wootie most of the day, reminding myself i had a place to stay if it got too cold. shout outs Fiona, really. she is more hospitable than i deserve. each place ive stayed in London has had washing and drying machines which is wild. howd i get so fucking lucky? when Wootie asks how i knew these people whove been generously letting me crash, simplest answer is friends of friends. exclusively people i had contact w thoo IG. globalization has made many things evolve and much arguably for the worse, but without widespread communication over the internet i would have spent every pound to my name on some hostel bed for 9 days and wouldnt eeem have the paper to buy food. i'm at a white Beatnik, i aint got any aunties to wire me cash when i'm down bad. feeling so inspired by these people, so in-love. although i felt some pinching guilt yesterday, which i rarely feel, yet thought about this time thanks to discussions w Deadbody about his Catholic upbringing. i smoke two struggle joints thoo-out the night, angling smoke outside the bedroom window, making sure to crane my arms and neck towards the outside to keep the room from reeking. despite best efforts the wind bullies a percentage of the smoke back into the room. i leave it open until me and Wootie finish fucking both times. i never asked about smoking in the house or let alone how Fiona felt about weed. guilt washes over me the higher i achieve. the room shares a wall w Fionas room. i go down Wootie for a grip both times because she had explained that the man she was seeing recently stopped eating her out and only wanted to fuck her during threesomes. hes missing out. she deserves head like the rest of us. the first time i came quick cuz i'm always quick. shout outs to my hella sensitive ass body. feel inches of ashamed that i came so quickly, disgusted w myself a bit yet leave that shit under wraps. after dinner and a couple drinks we walk back to the flat, copping some weed from some Egyptian kids on London Rd. i asked what language they were speaking as the kids disappeared into the darkness of an alleyway halfway down the street. it sounds so beautiful. 'Arabic. i'm Egyptian.' Fiona is definitely home the second go round. i implored Wootie to control her moaning. she commands my hand to her throat, yet that aint functionally halt a damn thing. i feel like i'm disrespecting Fiona but it didnt stop me. i snuggled w Wootie after and got her a tissue because i lied and said i didnt have anymore condoms so i hit it raw the second time. she and i talked about how we both been tested within the last week. guilt still, *the fuck is you doing*. i lied cuz i was being tepid bout fucking a second time, but she grabs my dick, grips and thumbs the head, stares unblinkingly at me w her wide, dead eyes. smile stretches a few centimeters, that odd, polite Canadian accent. only see teeth when sumn is LOL funnti. talks w an anxious sheepishness thats cute. all thoo-out our interactions i wonder what shell be a few years from now, when she sheds more of her small-townness and absorbs more of London.

keep it moving

iont understand how to navigate London; getting lost at every single turn today.

skkrt.

PERCEPTIBLE EFFECTS OF ALCOHOL ON MY BODY

- a haziness that clouds every thought
- omnipresent lethargy
- slowness
- theres scant wit or sharpness to everything so positivity is elusive
- omnipresent uncertainty
- a sterile taste in my brain, like everything is blank and interestless
- a loss of words like, yo i'm not hungover but i feel the alcohol in my blood

theres emptiness. moon coolin against the dark clouds *ta-dow* and the thundering of a military chopper. i'm blank on the inside because despite the fucking cold i'm aimlessly wandering Croydon for a few blocks sad af. i guess i'm tryna wander to find food or a snack or some shit but aint no fighting yfm. hoool'at down. if i can detach myself from this emptiness i can see new details in familiar environments. talk w Sophie about death, about my attitude towards death (she smiles cutely and tells me its bullshit). i tell her i'm not afraid to die, that ive made some peace. she aint never been Nigger. i'm lowkey ex-

cited to die—not that a nigger tryna rush shit. when i die illve fulfilled a complete life. we all deserve that completion. theres some catharsis there, somefuckingwhere. clearly i'd love a long life but its outta my hands.

skkr

getting nervous about going to Vienna because Natalie isnt answering any of my messages and iont know or have the ability to read German and have zero guwop for a hostel.

skkr

SOUNDS POST-APPLE-BONG

beautiful droning from the Sainsbury freezers. aggressive engines on the double decker buses.

skkr

A WALK, POST-GETTING BAILED ON

my espresso-splattered Doc Martens siftin kickin thoo dead leaves. smooth tyres on unfamiliarly shaped cars. sine waves from bus brakes. me humming Trippie and DRAMs *Ill NaNa.*

scuffing
scuffing
scuffing (yuh!)

the sticky stench of toxic fumes panics my central systems. a greyness in the creases of my right hand as i'm swypin. trees w tips dyed blonde. packs of lowly growling motorcycles. 'all buses, all tubes, all trains.' bodies, black in the nighttime, pressed against the black and gold gates peering into Buckingham Palace. subtle vibrations from the River Thames and constant traffic making Westminster Bridge feel like it may fall from beneath me—doesnt seem like all my steps are connecting.

skkrt to Austria

WIEN

the apartment in Vienna is mighty quiet, thinking about things that could get me deported. two days prior: i'm w S. (whomst is so so fine) and John in London, i'm a lil fay fay from a couple spliffs and a couple pints (context), and somehow, the subject of me not being afraid to get deported comes up. i remember i nearly miss a tap-in coming out of the Tube, i'm like *iont gih no fuKC that i missed that shit, DEPORT MY ASS!*—Yo also, i'm out chere in London hittin struggle joints and manmade fruit bongs on the street, lowkey strictly for IG, taking real risks—John and S. hold icy faces at my deportation joke. they wanna see my face always, they tell me selfishly, remind me that getting deported from a country like the United Kingdom would look terrible on my passport; i acquiesce, this is a very American attitude i'm expressing: that fearlessness movin thoo other countries, that confidence, that *arr*ogance. i'm not super proud to have boasted like that. the US is so fucking massive that i can identify that confidence in having to stay there cuz its Fucking America, giant fucking place, America is a hole like that though. damn near a jail cell itself.

i enter the wilderness of a dream, where i see myself walking thoo the streets of some ambiguous American city, walk by a man as he pulls out the lengthiest, six-shooter ive ever seen, the longboi breathes flames, i kiss low to the sidewalk near a fire truck where an undercover officer instructs me to stay low and out the street, dreamt-minutes pass, more officers run past me which i take as my signal to get the fuck off the streets for real so i run around the nearest corner, catch breath, hear a woman around my age tell her elder that 'Michael just tried to hit a lick,' a few feet away some skin is burning and irritated so i ask a woman on the street if i'm shot, she let me know theres just scrapes presumably from pressing my torso against the concrete for a lil grip but i'm almost sure i got grazed judging from the runway of skin missing from my right shoulder.

wake up following this dream feeling frenzied because so rarely do i dream so vividly, i know i'll have material for this next book. finally, some solid direction, i think. the next instant i check my phone and have a message from the New York State government with a determination that theyre withholding future unemployment payments because i'm outta the country, effectively leaving me broke in Europe for the next 15 days. one hour of tossing/turning. Natalie texts me to let her into her apartment. shes late to an appointment but i try to tell her the situation. she doesnt fully comprehend so tells me we'll talk about it later.

i drink coffee outta dirty mug, plug my phone into the speakers and Joni Mitchells *Be Cool4* plays automatically. easiest way to save money is to adopt a 'fuck food' attitude. 40€ to my name—scratch that, make that 39€.

---

[4] *If theres one rule to this game*
Everybodys gonna name
its be cool
If youre worried or uncertain
If your feelings are hurtin
Youre a fool if you can't keep cool
Charm em
Dont alarm em
Keep things light
Keep your worries out of sight
And play it cool
Play it cool
Fifty-fifty
Fire and ice

If your heart is on the floor
Cause youve just seen your lover
Comi through the door with a new fool

QUICK PLANS...

stop eating
begrudgingly ask parents for a lil guwop
~~fill out this questionnaire on the NYS government website~~
resist thinking about ramifications
resist thinking that without income rent is impossible
resist thinking that i'll have to move back to Kansas City
find ways to make some guwop young nigger

(*time passes*)

stress sleeping, veins screwed-up.

skkr

Be cool
Dont get riled
Smile—keep it light
Be your own best friend tonight
And play it cool
Play it cool
Fifty-fifty
Fire and ice

Dont get jealous
Dont get over-zealous
Keep your cool
Dont whine
Kiss off that flaky valentine
Youre nobodys fool
Be cool fool
Be cool
(Lots of other fish in the sea)

i take Natalies advice to go see the 16th district. searching for a Turkish coffee. walk along Brunnengasse like *phew*. cheap

clothing. halal meats. rabbits ducks chickens hanging from carts. go to a cafe outside Yppenpark where i get a 3,8€ Turkish coffee to warm my gloveless fingers. when told the price i hand the waitress 3€ because iont fully understand her—or i guess, any—German. ivé never felt more lonely and disconnected from anyone as much as i do from the cold, impatient eyes of the woman behind the counter. i get it but fuck breh. eatin these dreams. McDonalds is now THE viable food option.

skkr

Play it cool
Play it cool
Fifty-fifty
Fire and ice
So if theres one rule to this game
Everybody's gonna name
its—be cool

take the U2 to Donaumarina anticipating a nice walk. Google Maps leads me on a route down Otto-Futterknecht-Weg, which at first im like where tf you taking me nigger but i'm also like this shit knows the city better than me so i trust it. takes me down a gravel road behind some private residences, continuing underneath the Southeast Tangent where each concrete beam is tattooed w graffiti. i kick clouds of beige dirt and keep my eyes open to the possibility of loose, discarded euros. aint find shit though. on a road in Arenaweise. rows of leafless branches remind me of my hair, and knowing that imma tree from way back, i settle myself to the scenery, mirroring their ability. i hear birds i cant identify but they dont sound different than ones i'm used to. i fuck off the paved path straight into the woods where there are grassless strips from tires and foot traffic. i see a nigger (not a nigger really) practicing balancing on a tightrope. i think, '*damn*, i want some fucking weed.' wouldnt mind some auditory hallucinations or enhancements. tryna feel different. *be different.*

If youre worried or uncertain
If your feelings are hurtin
You're a fool if you can't keep cool
They want you to
Charm em
Dont alarm em
Keep things light
Keep your worries out of sight
And play it cool
Play it cool
Fifty-fifty
Fire and ice

ALL
CATS
ARE
BLACK

WHATEVERS LOST FINNA BE LOST YFM

—me again

having a musical night. first off, i'm so stressed out from being broke that i subconsciously thinkaboutdying several times several ways. but anyways. up in Musikverein for the Brussels Philharmonic which is pretty tight. i go live on IG because no photos or videos are allowed during the performance. bop thoo the first movement of *Cinderella* which is the third piece overall, sitting against the wall in the standing room area w my pink bandana tied around my face. only me and one other tourist manage to get away w capturing the expressly forbidden media. go w Martin and his friend Viktor around the corner for a beer w his family. he gives me advice about different mountains or forests for hiking within city limits. Kahlenberg is the most popular which i naturally reject but am convinced to actually take that route because of its famous view of the Danube. making mental notes. i ask the table questions about the history of Austria post-war that they aint teach us in the States. talk a bit about New York City, about how according to one of the family members its very very European, which i'm inclined to partially agree. our music is better. i spend gwop on two beers and am brought down mentally but hide that shit. we leave and the friend shows me directions to the Rhiz where Natalie is supposed to be. he works in education and politics. my hope is to work w arts and free programs for underseen Black artists. i pop up at the Rhiz to uninspiring electronic music. pretty slow for as fast as it pretends to be. Natalie fay fay and i'm tryna bop but cant get into it. i'm fucking bored, honestly. iont feel moved and i cant pretend to move. i'm spoiled being from the USA cuz we got the best music say dat! text to Deadbody and Peachcurls: *Europe is the Magna Carta of the world of music.* (if you know you know). just salty and hatin so what that mean? i sneak looks at Magda because she has the most beautiful eyes and demeanor. a dude dances w Natalie eeem after she lies to him that i'm her man. she strong and independent in the most serious of ways so i'm not at all worried about her, plus lowkey she be acting like she dont want my ass around. i linger just so no brazy bullshit jump off. back at Natalies flat, its 0200, i'm pissed that aint no food in the brib.

keep moving

IAM HERE, SOMEWHERE IN THE SUN

finally solidify plans w Alba from Tinder to link in Stadtpark. i choose that park purposefully cuz my roommate Lauranda supposedly left me something in a secret place. *Lil Scavenger Hunt: A Memoir.* have to break apart the clues she texted me—pinching in and out of Google Maps to see which park has a river runnin thoo it, busted that shit down a lil bit more, consulted the reference photo, then i'm like it has to be *there* yeah yeah fa sho. she damn near demanded i search for this shit when i got to Vienna. she was here like five or six weeks before ya boi. so i'm like bet that. i meet Alba outside Cafe Pruckel and we walk her bike into the park. we spot the statue of two nude male bodies attempting to move a rectangular boulder, one wrists and shoulders it while the other tryna twerk that bitch off the ground. beautiful; and funny as hell somehow. i examine all sides of the statue positioned above a fountain. Alba takes videos; i'm subconsciously really into only knowing her physically for 6 minutes and her being comfortable enough to flame my goofyass. i'm elbow-deep in rocks hoping to avoid spiders. examining graffiti. circlin circlin circlin. Alba pokes around while i'm texting Lauranda, pleading for clues. eventually she sends me additional reference photos revealing a cave and miniature waterfall adjacent to the homoerotic sculpture. the pictures take ages to download on this European phone signal—no WiFi in the park. i notice and comment on the enormous khaki-feathered black swans. like i'm easily astonished but these fucking birds breh breh are *massive*. Alba and i deep in mud tryna search for a clear ziplock baggie, both infinitely curious, both neeeed to know what this hunt will turn up. kids watching us. deadass, we search for like an hour before giving up and i'm theorizing there was never really anything there; the adventure could have been the whole point. 'you want to get a coffee?' she suggests the cafe where we met but she mentions its known to be homophobic, kicking out gay couples all the time. i'm like, lets have a walk. end up at her place because she wants soup after a discussion about how we both hate cold weather. 'i dont use the word *hate* too much, but i *hate* cold weather.' i concur. i mean i grew up where it snows in the winter so i'm used to it but i'm over allat snow etcetera damn near top of the season. love the fall, that cooling down from extreme warmth to the point i gotta wear a jacket or sweater, my body reacting differently under evolving environments, brain whippin, blood screwed, but when it drops below 45°—idkwtf that is in °C—i'm like *i get it*. Alba has a beautiful pre-war apartment in the 1st District that she pays so little for because her landlord—she babysits his kids—moved out after getting married. her room is big enough for a bed, a couch, a sewing desk, a cute ass bookshelf, and several decorative items. bedroom / workspace / relaxing space. ceilings high. she makes a miso soup w carrots and mushrooms and coriander and edamame. i make myself a sludgy coffee w an Italian coffeemaker. 'do you want to cut my hair?' i resist at first but she is so fucking cute and eeemno i'm nervous about destroying that thiccc curly mane i acquiesce. travel back in time to when i used to shave the side of Ricks head and help dye her hair. i ask Alba about her Kurdish background over lunch. we grind dried chilis into the soup which leads to stories about the street food i had in Chiang Mai in 2016. she offers me a pair of patiks her grandmother knitted for her which is sweet and eeen sweeter when she compliment how nice they look on me. the density of her arm hair is less forest-like than, say, my facial hair, yet dense enough to darken her skin. ranting about how i think hating a person based strictly on gender or skin color is childish and banal. i mean, *i get it.* its some evolutionary trait to be able to identify differences. i understand that you can subconsciously develop these prejudices because of the sociohistorical location but this just some socialized ideals thats *learned* and ~~*CAN*~~ **SHOULD** be **UNLEARNED**. hate me because i'm an asshole not because i'm Black or have dreads or tattoos or cuz i'm vulgar and beautiful—witcho hatin ass. she agrees, sees empathy actively oozing from my pores. post-soup she pours two glasses of white wine before i start chopping. 'maybe if i'm drunk i wont hate you if you mess up!' i'm solid under pressure, slide on my patiks and scuffle to her room, thow on some Yaeji while she sets up. pink bandana on my face praying silently to The Based God. 'i think that look suits you as *barber*'—theres a different word she uses. she holds just a few centimeters between her index- and middle fingers tryna demonstrate how much i should take off; gotchu. cut it. take my time and in about 6-7 minutes she says she likes it. 'oh it feels so short!' we sit knees touching on her white couch listening to Erykah Badu as i'm going thoo tagged IG photos of me pre-dreads. briefly use her three panel mirror to pick lint off the back of my head. already pre-decided i'm gonna cancel my other potential Tinder dates to make emotional time for Alba. 'what are you doing the rest of the days you are here?' i'm tryna drop hints. she has another Tinder date the tomorrow that i convince her to cancel selfishly so i can get more time. she tells me about some performances going on and we look up information and i silently decide i cant go because i'm so fucking broke. but imma figure this shit out. she has to leave to babysit so she doesnt come to the protests against the newly-elected, ultra right-wing government later tonight. i slip on slick polished marble steps, almost lose my life. she hooks herself to me for the remaining flights. hug at the corner. walking towards Ballhausplatz. i'm all fucked up because yall know that i feel my emotions on Ten. feel em physically. really sucks that iont live in Vienna because deadass i'd seriously pursue Alba. cant deny tangible connections. sad at the ephemeral nature of life as always but i cant do shit but enjoy what i can when i can.

yall feel me

how am i supposed to reflect and re-write a three-hours long conversation that felt like 30 minutes? is it worth it? is there any value in tracing pre-washed memories? i think theres real value in not fighting when you arent inspired.

skkrrr

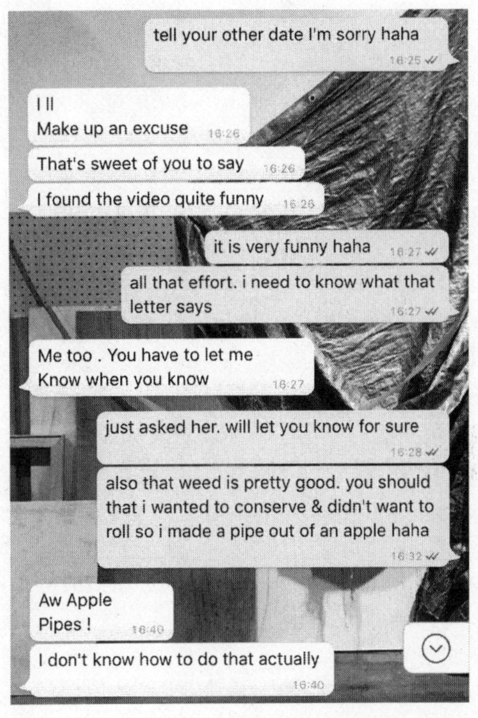
tell your other date I'm sorry haha
16:25
I ll
Make up an excuse
16:26
That's sweet of you to say
16:26
I found the video quite funny
16:26
it is very funny haha
16:27
all that effort. i need to know what that letter says
16:27
Me too . You have to let me
Know when you know
16:27
just asked her. will let you know for sure
16:28
also that weed is pretty good. you should that i wanted to conserve & didn't want to roll so i made a pipe out of an apple haha
16:32
Aw Apple
Pipes !
16:40
I don't know how to do that actually
16:40

the hardest thing about wanting to help somebody who doesnt want help is accepting and restraining yourself, allowing the person to ask for help when they comfortable asking and not imposing help onto them. its sad but like eeem though i do think me continually offering help in small ways to Alba like helping her pack or bringing her a coffee is positive, its only really sad in a self-serving way because i'm only tryna do that to see her one last time. its not about me. funny the point time at which you meet people in their lives. i'm not no shoulda-coulda-woulda type nigger. i look at workaway.info very briefly in Vienna to hold on to some fantasy of staying, but it makes me realize the logistical issues w tryna abruptly immigrate to another country. Milan will be incredible but that means imma finite number of days away from flying back to the United States where shit will be very real very immediately. i know its finna all work out but like how much of this trip is just me practicing my disappearing act?

skkr

i pack up my bags and get the fuck outta Natalie apartment before 1100, drink half a cup of day old coffee. have to take my full ass backpack to Kahlenberg cuz aint no coming back. *Bodega Boys* on the way up. at the top eyes follow the Danube slithering thoo Vienna. the skyscrapers are lower than ones i'm accustomed. eating a hot dog for energy before i hike down. its beautiful up here, the hike is beautiful. hike down a lil corniche path where the running stream and its *ssssss* against the reluctant breaking leaves soundtrack the scene. i'm stompin slidin and its kinda muddy so the Docs is slippin cuz my soles slick. when i'm certain i'm far enough from people i open the jar holding the weed Alba gave me that first night, pull out the remaining struggle joint and hit half. DM my niggers and crushes on IG. smoke stings my left eye. tfw youre hiking a large hill in East-Central Europe and youre far away from home and comforts. them Bronx hills were a good precursor to these inclines, i'm huffin / puffin, my heart leaps against my ribcage yet feels refreshing. when my backpack gets too heavy i pivot, peep alternate paths back—if i didnt have to leave tonight i would take another three hours to roam the entire path. i have search for stumps to plop on when i'm losing breath. hit that last lil half and vclose my eyes for a few minutes, processing the sound of the forest. rustling above me, spot a person squat-pissing against a dead bush. back at the top of the hill the cafe is too full so i hop on the bus back down to see if i can find my friend Spittas familys dedication plaque. i do find it, now have to find a pencil or some charcoal to make a rubbing. so sheepish when i'm tryna say anything in German.

skkrt to Italy

texts to Deadbody at passport control:

breh

they took everything out of all my bags & unrolled my jeans & checked all the pockets

in the de muerte sack too i had a jar w some weed crumbs in it

they let me hold it down

i checked the weed laws here though so i wasn't worried. best believe a nigga ain't gonna get caught up on no shit like that

the cops that checked were young & they smelled the jar & was like what was in this i said a little weed that i smoked w a friend & they laughed

waved over their superior who just like waved it off so i got to keep it

no eeem enough to pack Gilda (rip) so not worth they time

HOW TO UNQUALIFY YOURSELF AS A FRIEND OF MINE

CLOSED COMMUNICATIONS: aight so i know that for most people using language can be anxiety-inducing and i should have some knowledge in how to read your body language but if theres any bubbling, palpable uncomfortability then i NEED yall to tell me whats up. i love yall and could never hate yall, so please respect me by letting me know what problems you may be having w me so i can act accordingly. i personally cannot read your thoughts so clear, open, honest communication is key.

(i encourage the reader to add more here below, just to keep track for yallselves) the past and the future are both abstractions to me. the past is sumn i know ive lived thoo but as time treks omnidirectionally i will for sure recall it differently. not because my memories are fallible but because i'll have a different context to place it in. (photos / videos / media will fuck up that fallibility fa shoooooo.) the future is the future and while its not completely useless to plan for the future i do think its not worthwhile to *worry* about it. the present tense is the only valid reality that matters because its tangible. each second you should appreciate because its your only guwopportunity to do so and in this way you trick yourself into subconsciously appreciating every second in your life. the rest of that shit is just time travel convince me otherwise.

skkr

i'm tryna appropriate white male confidence because if they finna take something of ours its what i wanna take from them. this Deadbodys idea originally. theres real value in that. do shit w such unreasonable level of comfortability that any consequence is abstracted to the point of nonexistence.

skkr

Princeton University really fut up not giving me the Hodder Fellowship. i gotta get the fuKC outta my country for awhile cuzzo.

skkr

its funny being on the outside and not understanding Italian cuz its like less about the words and more about the sonic properties. i find that my emphatic gesticulations are most effective in achieving my point.

skkr

my poor brain is stressed in Milano. i can tell because last night i had several vivid dreams that tell me how fucking stressed i am subconsciously, w asking my Momma for money and giving Peachcurls my room for December cuz i have no income and not being able to pay Glowseph for my portion of the house bills and being rejected from Princetons Hodder bullshit and feeling so rejected by my own country. i'm keeping an eye open for any opportunity to stay in Milan. i break up a hash puck w my fingers and take a video of me rolling a struggle spliff in Fredi kitchen as i'm ruminating.

skrr skrr

DREAM #1: i'm in the middle of a paved street in the nighttime when i realize its definitely an American city, in my head in the dream i'm like *wait cuzzo you in Italy* so soon as i confirm this i have my very first lucid dream, immediately i try to fly and fail so i'm sawty and like what the fuck is the point lollll, i decide just to run but i can only run in near-slow motion, i'm okay w this though because i'm practice patience, Thank You Based God.

DREAM #2: i nearly have my first wet dream, never have had a wet dream because since like 14 my masturbation game been top tier, i'm in Fredi bed laying next to a person whose name is KC but it wasnt my great amazing beautiful friend KCV, we snuggin, my arms are ropes around them, my left thumb rubbing they nipples w some significant pressure, enough to elicit moaning, which is subdued cuz its dark and there are the assumed roommates but they grind that ass into me and wrap legs around mine and doesnt want me to stop…i wake up on my back and have to triple check my dick to see if i came which i didnt. but that shit was wild.

skkr

staring at the ceiling in Fredi room. one more week until shit gets real and i need to have a plan for how to get money rolling in once i'm stateside. really hoping some job, any fucking job at this point, comes calling.

skkr

a poem that says

WHAT DA FUKC IZ IMMA DO

6,000 times. its smacking on some *Mystic Stylez* type beat.

skkr

eat a panzerotti w Fredi and her friend in a square near Duomo di Milano. i have to kick at pigeons to keep em away, flinching

when they manically jump back flapping fervently. sitting in a university library wondering how people can study in here. yfm iont fw that open floorplan lifestyle, i need silence for concentration. (that ADHD dont play.) the bathroom doors slam and creak w consistency. coughing. i think about sculptures i'm tryna make. find a 1€ coin on the ground after i drop off G. at the metro. one horrible art-for-dummies gallery opening then one pretty cool one. G.s friends tell me to check out this residency that would teach me bronzeworking if i'm tryna move to Milan. decide to take the half hour walk home to save a trip on my ten-trip card. piss so good while i'm drunk it makes me wanna keep drinking.

skkr

REASONS WHY I FW SLEEP HEAVY

1. you need a fair amount of it to function at capacity
2. its essentially escapism

yall ever think maybe people aint really tryna function at capacity?

skkr

i get mad sad following a conversation about body hair w G. and Fredi during an aperitivo. its 5€ cuz its Black Friday. maybe that was just for me. pretty much i start feeling sad when G. talks about hating her body hair and a broader conversation is sparked after i say i would take pubic hair over smoothness any day of the week. 'in Italy, a man will not be attracted to a woman w leg hair.' i flagrantly call bullshit because i'm deeply against a person who decides another persons attractiveness is devalued by something natural that we all share. i mean do you, i'm just saying miss me w that concept. if you grow hair and you personally dont like it on your body its your body and your decision but fuck someone shaming you for these qualities. 'Americans are rebellious.' *si.* i talk about the 1960s. i drunkenly talk about how America is born from revolution so its just in us culturally. the Aperol spritz hits. but i'm sad because shes stubborn and she eeem acknowledges this. its bullshit to be judged based on this but its "part of our culture" so "what can you do?" i'm trying not to be visibly affected but yall know my animated face ass. i think about how i shouldnt just accept some shit in a culture just for the cultures sake. fuck being passive yfm. i think about if slaves were that passive, where i would be rn? i think about cultures who stone women who dont wrap they heads up. should people just accept shit? culture constantly changes because people change, worlds change. iont believe in letting somebody control how you see yourself. i'd rather be alone. iont fw limiting yourself based on someone elses opinion. your body is all you have absolute control of; you have no choice but to inhabit this muhfucka. i concede though i'm being a lil bit idealistic and judgmental especially because this is my first trip to Italy. what in the literal fuck do i know? maybe some people work well w limitations. i just hate to see people i love submitting to what another person thinks in a way that affects their behavior in a seemingly negative way. detrimental to your mental, ofttimes physical, health. all for something you can do nothing about. seems sus. seems like sumn i *shouldnt* fw.

skkr

me and Fredi only talk in our private meow-meow language after her cocktail.

skkr

PCP[5]

i keep staring off to test if i smoked angel dust or not,people pouring beers into each other cups,mighty warm in this shit, mighty warm in nis bih,i assume that Fredi is dead when she outta eyesight,tryna remember images like a muhfucka.

dont be rude bousin get hit w some secret special metal i aint expect after dissociating for hellas and work this neck out bb, MAH WANT ME TO MILLY ROCK FA HER, imagine me clapping my hands tween each syllable, imagine a kebab white sauce all on that shit but like yogurty instead of thicc like mayonnaise.'we are the party.'—giulia, smacking the steering wheel.

skkr

---

[5] aight so boom, travelling back in time to that time i accidentally smoked PCP. i really almost let that slide past yall, but if i'm judging w my contemporary eye, its a story i come back to whenever i describe this time in my life. always w time—Time be hazy. but aight: Fredi and G. take me to this club that from what i remember started w people squatting and throwing parties and eventually they acquired the space by just staying. so we enter, the main room is large ballroom w a coffered dome, high dark in all corners, pale blue light from the corner perpendicular to the entrance, drony / noisy music plays w the faintest rhythm at a level thats uncomfortable. tables lining remaining walls facing the makeshift stage. stiff, rusty light at the far back wall. ive been smoking on and off all day, drank a few Campari spritz, chillin. i have to piss, we head to one side of the stage into a secondary room, darker than the first, black-black-black, only dingy light source coming from the bathroom. mans is standing close to the stalls and speaking English to people waiting in line, dreaded like me, i catch his eyes and smile-nod, ask him what he smoking on. 'its the ganja man,' passes it to me. i thank him cuz flower real hard to come

SOUNDS OF MY LAST LONG WALK IN MILAN

its funny how all human languages sound the same when enough people are talking simultaneously. smooth tires same lil shit. someone rapping en Italiano, riding a skateboard. dead leaves on a dirty ground. emerald-headed ducks causing ripples in the water. cloudless, blue af sky. kids climbing over stone barriers to cast lines. music all along the river—a drummer plays along to some unrecognizable song—wait they actually playing *Fireworks* but Katy Perry, thats tight. a little girl has a coat the same faded military-green as the one on my body but w pink fur helmeting the hood. *Always Free* spray painted in silver. *scusa mi*. i'll always remember buying hash from some Arab teenagers in Colonne de Lorenzo, watching them almost take a metal stanchion to some tourists for poppin they mouth. *ssst sttt*, 'ciao boss.' 'no grazie.' i got what i needed. thank you.

---

by out here. he calls me Bob Marley, lets me piss before him. on my way out into darkness my eyes adjust slowly to the weed and the absence of light when mans waves me to him and his boys posted to the wall, blending in sans teeth. mans tells me he has anything i need, 'Cocaine, MD, whatever you need,' 'i'm broke family, but i really appreciate it. i would if i could,' 'where you live?' 'New York City,' 'You got money up there man!' 'You as in white people, i *pay* money to be there, aint got nothing left.' its all good he tells me, lets me hold down the remainder of the joint. while facing said joint i start feeling floaty and looser. mans is from Gambia, starts telling me about Kunta Kinte and the origins of the slave trade in Gambia, going off—but so then he pats himself down, daps me up while drawing me close to his chest, i aint afraid of any embrace yfm, pushes me away and says he need to go see his man about some more dust— nigger excuse me? i think of dust and then i think of Angel Dust. i feeling a lil different, like high but like high-high-high, disconnected from my extremities. i have to warn Fredi and G. then explain what PCP is. i float away for a few moments, then the above happens.

skkr

the most consistent thing around is inconsistency.

skkr

this is my last night in Milan, my second date w Acid Eyes. we meet at Isola after my last long walk. G. meets back for one last hug before returning home to practice w her band for the night. too sentimental; i gotta see muhfuckas walk away as a possible last memory. Acid Eyes locks up her bike off by SPRINT, which i didnt expect to be a zine fest. end up seeing a press that follows me on IG so i'm plottin, spend the €2,50 i got on a lil beer to ignore large crowd anxieties. meet the people who run Friends Make Books, dudes from New York and we bond over my idea of Milan being similar to NYC, like being cool without really flaunting. it just exists. me and Acid Eyes make our way around but its sweltering in this bitch and she agrees we should dip out. lil cigarette and one more round thoo the fest. i stop by an Indian spot down the street for a lil kebab and some big conversation about race and gun laws in the United States. i talk briefly about Chicago and my empathy towards all the ways people suffer there, and how i'm not tryna fantasticize the environment because shit be really really real. (shout outs all the gang members i know surviving, love and respect to yall.) i lead this conversation into one about acquiring face tattoos, naturally. very close; please remember i do everything i say imma do. after eating we walk for a grip in the crippin ass cold to find a decent aperitivo to eat more and i want one final Aperol Spritz before i'm up out this shit tomorrow, since i'm prolly not drinking once in the States. Pub 24 is a lowkey come up and the music is good—okay but sidenote my only complaint here is that they cut off *Bank Account* before the verse. And like they were actively playing rap-esque shit: *XO Tour Llif3*, some reggaeton and Italian trap. so why hate on 21 Savage? we theorize about why of all songs, that one was singled out. *thats enough!* head ass. 'All i can think of is like its a hit but yeah its like very Rap and mad vulgar.' 'But most people wont know the words in English, so i dont know.' expansion, debate. head out, get lost searching for her bike but stop for a gelato cuz its so cold. i speak laughably bad Italian tryna order but the counterperson thinks its cute and picks up what i'm putting down enough for it to be a successful transaction. funny enough we hear 21 Savages verse on *Rockstar* while we eat. wandering cute ass sidewalkless backstreets, tryna direct me to the Green Line. 'can i kiss you?' she staggers a bit, flattered, i misread and think its a *no* but she says its sweet because

nobody ever *asks* her. so i creep up and we make out for like 20mins. she's stunned-still, and i'm like, sheeeit, 'yo so do you live far...cuz i can come over *for a lil bit* at least.' 'its not far but its not close...' some hesitation because she has some writing to do so i'm like its cool. her skull holds adorable sad sleepy eyes and a smile she doesnt let most people see. so we break away and i head to Fredis sawty that i'm ending the night bunless, but Acid Eyes and the date itself is something i'll forever hold precious. i have to pack up all my shit. i aint got no weed.

gonna hit this sleep and wake up early. sawty i'm leaving Milan. i'll be back in this shit fa sho though beleeedat.

skkr

mountains considering the sunlight outside the Milano-Bergamo airport. frozen dew got patches of grass looking white from the bus window. J Dillas *Delights Vol. I* cuz i cant download the PBS Newshour fully.

skkrrrrr

back in New York City, back coolin on the couch cuz i'm temporarily taking over the living room. i make a cozy fort from the big cushions to block out the sunlight. watching *Lost*, listening to the sucking, grindin, whirlin sounds emanating from project pipes. move rooms to Lauranda bed while she was out dancing, staring at the ceiling, not sleeping, thinking about how i'll never be loved by people the way i love them. thats some ol mopey bullshit though. i'm just like chalk fulla cum and thinkindreaminboutfucking. the most househusbandy shit i thought just now: i wish i had a three-compartment sink so i can restaurant-quality-wash these dishes; what happiness that would bring me. scrollin thoo Netflix lit, strugglin to make a decision because iont wanna get too inspired and not be able to fall asleep. everybody please give yourself a round of applause for holding yourself back when it be like that. we all deserve that.

skkrt.

its funny that i had suuuch muhfuckin confidence that when i got back to New York i could slide and stay at a lil sumn sumn lil crib. everybody is presently working on them. whats a less pathetic way of asking, 'can i sleep in your bed w you so i dont have to sleep on the couch in my own damn apartment?' i like to think i'm not terrible company. i like to think hella shit as yall know. couch is cool, i have shelter. been caught these couches before. shout outs impromptu sleepovers at Deadbodys set. shout outs to my people for knowing exactly what i need.

since its cold in the crib and i'm thinkinboutdyin, i sleep a lil deeper. certain situations dont have no business changing, damn near.